Lost in
the Clouds

Tom Tinn-Disbury

There was a boy named Billy and he loved his mommy very much.

She loved Billy very much, too.

But the trouble was,
Billy's mommy died.

He liked to think she
was now in the clouds.

Billy didn't like Mommy being in the clouds,
but it wasn't a big problem all the time.

Each morning Billy would go to
his bedroom window to check
how Mommy's cloud was doing.

He would often imagine what
it was like up on her cloud.

Some days, when the sky was clear and blue, Billy and Daddy would play in the yard until they were both too tired to play any more.

These were the
best days.

Billy knew that
Mommy had asked
the sun to make
their days bright.

Then there were days when Mommy's cloud filled the sky but stayed a nice, bright white.

On these days, because her cloud was bigger, Billy felt Mommy was closer. He would talk to her, but sometimes that just made him miss her more.

Daddy wasn't quite the same on these days. He would be quieter and his eyes would always be looking far away, as if he was trying to find Mommy in the distance somewhere.

Then there were
the *really bad days.*

Billy could always sense the rumbles
overhead and could see the sky getting darker.

Mommy's cloud would be so big
and dark, hanging heavy in the
sky. Billy would then feel the
raindrops plop onto his forehead.

Billy would try to talk to Mommy, but the

howling wind, driving rain,
and
thunderous rumbles

made it almost impossible to hear anything.

Billy would have to

scream and

shout.

These were the days Billy really needed his daddy, but Daddy would be quiet, and his eyes would look red and sore.

The best thing for Billy to do was sit peacefully, close his eyes tight, and hope things would brighten up soon.

It was one of those stormy, thundery days.

Billy was fed up of knowing his mommy was only just above him, but he couldn't see or be with her. He decided to climb up to her clouds, so that he could talk to her.

Billy knew it would be tough.

The clouds were far away, but with enough things stacked on top of each other and with Daddy's ladder from the shed, he believed he could do it.

Billy piled boxes, books, and pots as high as could be.

Then he fetched the ladder and placed it on top.

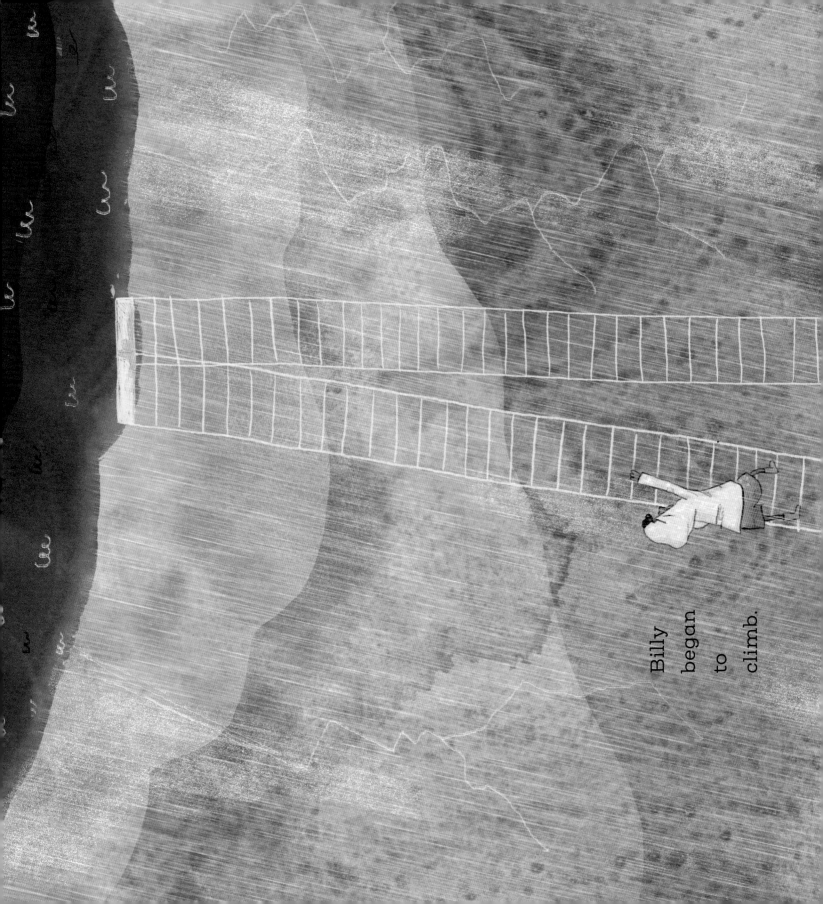

Billy
began
to
climb.

The wind howled in his ears. The rain stung his cheeks and the cold went straight through to his bones.

Billy shouted as loud as he possibly could for his mommy. He was desperate for her to hear him. But the rain and wind became too much.

Billy slipped.

It felt like he was falling forever.

Then, with an

OmpH

he was caught.

Billy opened his eyes.

"Hello, Munchkin," Daddy said.

"Hello, Daddy," Billy sniffed.

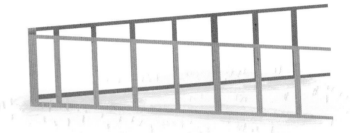

Daddy placed Billy
on his feet, knelt down,
and gave his son the
biggest, squeeziest hug
he had felt in a long time.

"What were you doing climbing the ladder, Billy?" asked Daddy.

"I miss Mommy and I wanted to climb up to her clouds so that I could talk to her," said Billy, looking at his feet.

"You know, I miss Mommy a lot, too" said Daddy. "But when I do, I find talking to her makes me feel a bit better. I like to tell her about my day and all about you, Billy.

You can speak to her, too. You could talk to her when you're in bed, at school, or just playing in the yard."

"Sometimes I feel really sad, Daddy," said Billy.

"It's okay to feel sad, confused, scared, or angry, Billy,
especially when we loved Mommy so much" said Daddy.

"I sometimes feel sad and angry, but you can always talk to people about how you're feeling. You have lots of people who love you and will listen to you. Your aunts and uncles, Mommy's friends, your teacher, and, of course, you can talk to me anytime.

We can talk about the fun memories we have of Mommy. Or, even if you just want a hug, I am always here for you."

"I love you, Daddy," said Billy.
"Love you too, Munchkin," said Daddy.

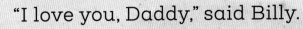

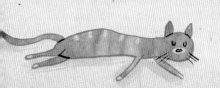

As if by magic, the rain disappeared, the sky became clearer, and a spectacular rainbow stretched across the sky.

Something in the yard caught Billy's eye.
He saw the most beautiful flower.

It was tall, colorful, and full of
life. Billy had planted it with
his mommy, but that was a
long time ago.

He hadn't realized how much
it had grown since then.

"The rain from Mommy's thundercloud helped it grow," said Billy.

"That's right. Something beautiful can grow in the stormiest weather," said Daddy. "We will plant a new flower next to it and they can grow together, side by side."

Knowing that Mommy was watching over them from her cloud, Billy and Daddy could now brave the thunderstorms together.

Guide for Grown-Ups

Going through grief can be hard, especially when your child is going through it, too. Here is some advice on how to manage the situation with your little one:

What should I tell my child?

- Try to be as honest and open as possible about what has happened.

- Use simple, age-appropriate language to explain everything, and break it down so that it is easier for your child to understand.

- Listen to your child. It's okay if you don't have all of the answers right now, but it is important that they feel supported and heard by you.

- Make sure that they know that they can talk to you, or others if they would prefer, at any time.

What else can I do to help them?

- Seek professional support if you are worried about your child.

- Remember, it is ok to cry and show your emotions in front of them. This shows them that you are grieving too, and encourages them to share their emotions with you.

- Children like routine, so try to keep things as normal as possible. But make sure that you also have some fun together.

- Talk about the person who has died. It can be nice to share memories with each other, and commemorate birthdays and other significant dates.

Resources:

- The Dougy Center - An organization that provides support to both adults and children who are experiencing grief.

- Actively Moving Forward - An app that provides teens with a network where they can feel connected and understood by young people who are going through a similar loss. It offers support groups, videos, comment boards, and allows its members to chat with each other.

- Family Lives On - An organization for children whose mother or father have died, which understands the importance of continuing family traditions that were celebrated with their deceased parent.

- The National Alliance for Grieving Children (NAGC) - a nonprofit organization that raises awareness about children and teens who are grieving the loss of someone close to them. It also provides education and resources for parents and other caregivers.

Penguin Random House

Created for DK by Plum5 Ltd

Consultant Stacey Hart
Editor Abi Luscombe
Designer Brandie Tully-Scott
US Senior Editor Shannon Beatty
Publishing Manager Francesca Young
Managing Editor Laura Gilbert
Jacket Coordinator Isobel Walsh
Publishing Director Sarah Larter
Creative Director Helen Senior
Production Editor Dragana Puvadic
Production Controller Francesca Sturiale

First American Edition, 2021
Published in the United States by
DK Publishing
1745 Broadway, 20th Floor, New York,
NY 10019

Copyright © 2021
Dorling Kindersley Limited
DK, a Division of Penguin Random House
Company LLC
22 23 24 25 10 9 8 7 6 5 4
005–323173–May/2021

A CIP catalogue record for this book is
available from the British Library.
ISBN: 978-0-7440-3659-6

Printed and bound in China

MIX
Paper from
responsible sources
FSC™ C018179

For the curious

www.dk.com

About Tom Tinn-Disbury

Tom Tinn-Disbury is an author and illustrator living in Warwickshire, England. He lives with his wife and two children, and he is helped by his dog Wilma and cat Sparky.

Tom tries to give his characters rich, full lives, making sure they have a real range of feelings and emotions. That was particularly important in creating this book.

Tom would like to dedicate this book all the essential workers that help us in our day to day lives.

For Tracy, may you now be at peace.

About Stacey Hart

Stacey Hart is a therapist, trainer, university lecturer, and group facilitator. An expert on childhood bereavement and family breakdown, Stacey works as a trauma specialist in schools and corporations. She has also won a Family Law Award for best support services.

Stacey has appeared a number of times on television and radio as a leading voice on children's bereavement.

Bereaved children like Billy have taught her to hold hope, and live every day to the fullest.